New Blue Shoes

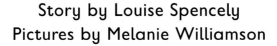

Story by Louise Spencely
Pictures by Melanie Williamson

OXFORD
UNIVERSITY PRESS

Ella put on her blue shoes.
They were too small.

2

"My blue shoes are too small," said Ella.

"We will get you some new blue shoes," said Grandpa.

Grandpa and Ella went into a shoe shop.

There were some yellow shoes,
but there were no blue shoes.

So they went into the
next shop.

They saw some pink shoes,
but no blue shoes.

In the next shop there were some red shoes.

"These are red shoes,"
said Ella.

"But I want blue shoes," said Ella.

So they went into the
last shop.

The last shop was FULL of
blue shoes.

But which shoes did
Ella choose?